영어로 읽는 세계명작
Story House

THE V

3 백조왕자

Hans Christian Andersen

WorldCom Edu

Adapted by **Lori Olcott**
Illustrated by **Son Jin-Hee**

Published in Korea in 2003 by WorldCom Edu

Printed and distributed by WorldCom Edu

작가와 작품

안델센(Hans Christian Andersen, 1805 ~ 75)은 덴마크의 가난한 가정에서 태어나 제대로 배우지도 못했으나, 어릴 적부터 문학에 눈을 떴다. 생활이 곤란한 형편이었으나, 문학에의 간절한 소망과 타고난 소질, 그리고 소박하고 순진한 성격으로 많은 후원자를 찾아냈다. 1833년 이탈리아 여행의 인상과 체험을 바탕으로 창작한 『즉흥시인』으로 그의 이름이 유럽 전체에 퍼졌다. 같은 해에 내놓은 최초의 『동화집』은 그의 동화작가로서의 생애의 출발점이 되었다. 그의 동화의 특색은 서정적인 정서와 아름다운 환상의 세계, 그리고 따스한 휴머니즘으로 정리할 수 있다.
주요 작품으로는 『성냥팔이 소녀』 『벌거벗은 임금님』 『인어공주』 등이 있고 모두 130편 이상의 주옥 같은 책을 펴냈다.

작품 설명

새엄마(여왕)에 의해 성에서 쫓겨난 엘리스는 백조의 모습으로 변한 오빠들을 구하기 위해 벙어리로 지내야만 하는 상황에서 급기야 마녀로까지 몰리게 된다. 이처럼 힘든 상황에서도 자신의 뜻을 굽히지 않고 꿋꿋이 견뎌내는 엘리스의 모습은 안델센 자신의 힘들었던 시절을 반영했다고 할 수 있다. 안델센 동화의 특징은 민화와 설화를 중심으로 이루어졌지만 작가 자신의 자전적 요소가 강하다는 점이다.

Introduction

Hello, and thank you for your interest in Worldcom's Story House! I hope you and your children enjoy the stories and characters we present to you here.

These Fairy tales have been passed down from parent to child for generations and generations. They usually teach a lesson. They teach the values that are important in every culture; like being kind, generous and helpful to others. They show that looks can be deceiving. Something beautiful, can be cruel and evil. But something ugly, can be good and loving. They also teach the value of patience. Rewards for good deeds don't always come quickly. But be patient, and the good deeds you do will bring good deeds to you. And if you keep working hard, your efforts will pay off.

I have tried my best to re-tell these stories in modern and natural English, without being too complicated or too hard. Most middle school children can read these stories. But I hope that parents and other adults will enjoy reading these books with their children too. There are interesting parts in each story. I hope there is enough that everyone will enjoy reading the story and listening to the native speakers.

Again, thank you for joining us in Story House. We hope you enjoy your stay.

Zoo

이 책을 펴내며

안녕하세요. 월드컴의 Story House에 오신 것을 환영합니다. 부디 여러분과 여러분의 자녀들이 이 책이 들려주는 이야기들을 만끽하시길 바랍니다.

이 동화들은 부모에서 아이들에게로 여러 세대에 걸쳐 전해내려 온 이야기로서 교훈을 담고 있습니다. 이웃에게 친절하고 서로 도우면서 아낌없이 베푸는 것, 이러한 가치관의 중요성을 일깨워 주죠. 이러한 것들은 때때로 반대로 표현되기도 합니다. 겉보기에는 아름답지만 잔인하고 사악할 수 있으며, 비록 흉칙하게 보여도 착하고 사랑을 베푸는 사람일 수 있다는 것입니다. 이러한 이야기들은 우리에게 인내의 가치를 일깨워 주기도 합니다. 선한 행동의 대가는 그 즉시 되돌아오지 않습니다. 그러나 참고 기다린다면, 여러분의 선한 행동은 보답을 받을 것입니다. 그리고 열심히 노력한다면 그에 상응하는 결과를 얻을 것입니다.

저는 이 이야기들을 너무 복잡하거나 어렵지 않도록 현대적이고 자연스러운 영어로 전달하기 위해 최선을 다했습니다. 이 책은 중학교 수준의 학생이라면 누구든지 읽을 수 있습니다. 그러나 부모님을 비롯한 모든 이들이 자녀분들과 함께 이 책을 즐길 수 있기를 바랍니다. 이야기마다 제각기 재미있는 부분들이 있습니다. 네이티브들이 들려주는 생생한 이야기는 현장감을 더해 주어 자신도 모르는 사이에 동화세계에 빠져들게 될 것임을 믿어 의심치 않습니다.

다시 한 번 저희 Story House에 오신 것을 감사드리며, 계속 많은 사랑 부탁드립니다.

Lori Olcott

등장인물 주요 등장 인물

엘리스

새로 맞이한 새 여왕에 의해 성에서 쫓겨나오다시피 하여 여왕의 마법에 걸린 오빠들을 구하기 위해 위험을 무릅쓰게 된다.

여왕

엘리스의 새엄마이자 왕비, 동시에 강력한 마법을 쓰는 마녀이기도 하다. 엘리스를 성에서 쫓아내고 왕자들에게 마법을 건다.

이웃나라 왕자

사냥하던 도중에 엘리스를 발견하여 자신의 성으로 데려가지만 의심많은 대신의 농간으로 엘리스를 의심하게 된다.

수석 대신

의심이 많아 엘리스의 일거수 일투족을 지켜보다 결국에는 엘리스를 마녀로 몰아세운다.

엘리스의 11명의 오빠들

엘리스의 11명의 오빠이자 왕자들. 여왕의 마법에 의해 백조로 변하게 된다.

그 외의 등장 인물

왕과 그의 신하

노파

요정과 사냥꾼

감옥의 경비병들

Contents

SH-03-C
MP3

Chapter 1

Once upon a time, there was a king. He had eleven handsome sons and one beautiful daughter. The daughter's name was Elise. One day, he called all his children together.

once upon a time 옛날 옛적에
king 왕
have(-had-had) 가지고 있다
eleven 십일(11)
handsome 잘생긴
son 아들
beautiful 아름다운
daughter 딸
name 이름
one day 어느 날, 하루는
call together 불러모으다
children 아이들

★★★★★★★★★★★

Once upon a time, there was a king.
옛날 옛적에 한 왕이 살고 있었습니다.

One day, he called all his children together.
하루는 왕이 아이들을 모두 불러모았습니다.

Children, three years ago, your mother died. We all loved her very much. But the kingdom needs a queen. I met a wonderful woman. I asked her to marry me, and she said yes. She will be your new mother.

Is she beautiful?

Yes, she's very beautiful.

Is she smart?

Yes, she's very smart.

Is she kind?

Yes, she's very kind. I'm sure she will love you all. Please help me make her happy.

We will, Father!

★★★★★★★★★★★

I asked her to marry me, and she said yes.
그녀에게 나와 결혼해 달라고 부탁했더니 그녀가 승락했단다.

Please help me make her happy.
부디 내가 그녀를 행복하게 해줄 수 있도록 도와다오.

three years ago 3년 전에
mother 어머니
die(-died-died) 죽다
love 사랑하다
very much 아주 많이
kingdom 왕국
need 필요하다
queen 여왕
meet(-met-met) 만나다
wonderful woman 멋진 여자
ask 부탁하다
marry 결혼하다
say(-said-said) 말하다
new 새로운
smart 영리한, 머리가 좋은
kind 친절한, 상냥한
sure 확신하는
help 돕다
make ~을 …하게 하다
happy 행복한, 기분좋은
father 아버지

The next week, the new queen came to the castle. She was very beautiful and very smart, but she was not kind at all.

Husband, who are all these children?

They are my sons and my daughter. Children, say hello to your new mother.

Hello. Pleased to meet you.

I hate children. Keep them in their rooms.

But, my dear, everyone loves my children. They can't stay in their rooms all the time.

Then keep them away from me. I never want to see them. Especially the little girl. I hate little girls the most of all.

★★★★★★★★★★

Keep them in their rooms. 아이들을 방 안에 붙들어 두세요.

They can't stay in their rooms all the time.
아이들을 항상 방 안에 있도록 할 수는 없소.

next week 다음 주
come(-came-come) to …에 오다
castle 성
not … at all 전혀 …않다
husband 남편, 여보
say hello to …에게 인사하다
pleased 기쁜, 즐거운
meet 만나다
hate 싫어하다
keep in 가두다, 붙들어 두다
room 방
dear 여보, 아가(사랑하는 사람)
everyone 모두, 누구나
stay 머물다
all the time 항상, 늘
keep away 가까이 못하게 하다
never 결코 …않다
especially 특히
most of all 가장[특히] …하다

Elise ran to her room. She was crying. She was so sad that the queen hated her. Soon her brothers came to see her.

 It’s ok, Elise. Don’t cry. We love you.

 Why does the queen hate us so much?

 I don’t know. But we won’t let her hurt you.

 No, we won’t. John had an idea.

run(-ran-run) to …로 달려가다
cry 울다
sad 슬픈
soon 곧, 이윽고
brother 오빠, 남동생
see 보다
ok 괜찮은

why 왜, 어째서
know 알다
won’t will not의 줄임말
let …하게 하다
hurt 다치게 하다
have(-had-had) 가지고 있다
idea 생각, 아이디어

★★★★★★★★★★

She was so sad that the queen hated her.
그녀는 여왕이 자신를 싫어한다는 것이 너무 슬펐습니다.

But we won’t let her hurt you.
하지만 우리는 여왕이 너를 해치지 못하도록 할 거야.

John had an idea. 존에게 좋은 생각이 있어.

Tell Father that you want to live in the country with Aunt Mina. She will take care of you.

We can visit you on weekends, and you will be safe from the queen there. She scares us. We don't like her.

Thank you so much. I will do that.

want to …하고 싶다
live in …에 살다
country 나라
aunt 숙모, 아주머니
take care of …을 돌보다
on weekends 주말에
safe from …으로부터 안전한
there 그곳에서
scare 두려워하다
so much 너무, 대단히

★★★★★★★★★★★

Tell Father that you want to live in the country with Aunt Mina.
네가 아버님께 미나 숙모가 계신 곳에서 함께 살고 싶다고 말씀드리는 거야.

you will be safe from the queen there.
그곳이라면 여왕으로부터 안전할 거야.

The next morning, Elise found the king.

Father, may I ask you for a favor? I want to live with Aunt Mina in the country.

Why do you want to do that?

The queen doesn't like me. If I stay, she will be angry all the time. If I go, maybe she will be happier here.

I think you are right. I'm sorry to cause so much trouble for you.

It's alright, Father. I like Aunt Mina. And my brothers will visit on weekends. I will be very happy there.

★★★★★★★★★★★★

If I go, maybe she will be happier here.
만일 제가 가면 아마 어머니께서는 이곳에서 더 행복하실 거예요.

I'm sorry to cause so much trouble for you.
너를 너무 힘들게 해서 미안하구나.

next morning 다음 날 아침
find(-found-found) 찾다
ask for a favor …에게 부탁을 하다
stay 머물다
angry 화내다
all the time 항상, 늘
maybe 아마도

happier (happy의 비교급)더 행복한
think 생각하다
right (얘기가)맞는
sorry 미안한, 후회하는
cause trouble for
…에게 폐를 끼치다
alright 괜찮은

That afternoon, Elise left the castle. Everyone was sad to see her go, except the queen. The queen smiled. That night, the queen called for the eleven brothers.

Boys, I'm sorry. I was very mean to you when we first met. Let's be friends.

We thought you hated children.

that afternoon 그 날 오후
leave(-left-left) 떠나다
castle 성
everyone 모두, 모든 사람
sad 슬픈
except …을 제외하고
smile 미소짓다
night 밤
call for …을 큰소리로 부르다
eleven brothers 11명의 형제들
boys 아이들
mean 비열한, 심술궂은
first 처음으로
meet(-met-met) 만나다
let's …하자
friend 친구
think(-thought-thought) 생각하다
hate 싫어하다
children 아이들

★★★★★★★★★★★

Everyone was sad to see her go, except the queen.
여왕을 제외하고는 모든 사람들이 엘리스가 떠나는 것을 슬퍼했습니다.

I was very mean to you when we first met.
우리가 처음 만났을 때 내가 너희들에게 너무 못되게 굴었구나.

Let's be friends. 친하게 지내자.

We thought you hated children.
우리는 당신이 아이들을 싫어한다고 생각했지요.

I hate children who are loud and run around. But you are polite and quiet. I think I will like you. Let's have a picnic tomorrow. We will go to the lake to have lunch. We can talk and become friends.

Ok. We will have lunch with you tomorrow. Thank you.

(whispering) That was very strange.
Do you trust her?

(whispering) No, I don't trust her.
But we can't say no to the queen.
Let's be careful tomorrow.

loud 시끄러운, 떠드는
run around 이리저리 뛰어다니다
polite 공손한, 예의바른
quiet 조용한, 얌전한
have a picnic 소풍가다
tomorrow 내일
lake 호수
have lunch 점심을 먹다
talk 이야기하다
become friends 친구가 되다
whisper 속삭이다
strange 이상한
trust 믿다, 신뢰하다
say no 안 된다고 말하다
careful 주의 깊은, 조심하는

★★★★★★★★★★★

I hate children who are loud and run around.
난 시끄럽고 뛰어다니는 아이들을 좋아하지 않는단다.

But we can't say no to the queen.
하지만 여왕한테 안 가겠다고 말할 수는 없잖아.

Comprehension

Checkup I

I True or False

1. The king had twelve children.
2. The children's mother ran away.
3. The children loved the new queen.
4. The queen was sad to see Elise go.
5. The queen called for the boys.

II Multiple Choice

1. Which was not true about the new queen?

a. She was very beautiful.
b. She was very smart.
c. She was very kind.

2. What did the queen think about the children?

a. She loved them.
b. She hated them.
c. She didn't care.

정답은 p.116에

3. Where did Elise want to live?

a. She wanted to live with her Aunt Mina.
b. She wanted to live by herself.
c. She wanted to live in the castle.

4. Where did the queen want to go with the boys?

a. She wanted to ride horses through the forest.
b. She wanted to take a trip to the ocean.
c. She wanted to go on a picnic by the lake.

5. Why did the boys agree to go with the queen?

a. Because they could not say no to the queen.
b. Because they trusted her.
c. Because they wanted to be friends.

III Fill in the Blanks - use the words in the word bank

(each word is used once)

brothers	children	hurt	loud	marry
rooms	stay	weekends	won't	yes

1. I asked her to _____ me, and she said _____.

2. They can't _____ in their _____ all the time.

3. But we _____ let her _____ you.

4. And my _____ will visit on _____.

5. I hate _____ who are _____ and run around.

정답은 p.116에

IV Draw a line to connect the first half of each sentence with the second half:

A		B
Elise	•	• had an idea.
The kingdom	•	• was sorry to cause Elise trouble.
John	•	• needed a queen.
Aunt Mina	•	• was the only daughter.
The king	•	• lived in the country.

SH-03-C
MP3

Chapter 2

The next day, the queen and the brothers went to the lake. It was a beautiful day. It was sunny, and the birds were singing in the trees. The lunch was delicious.

These cookies are great. What are they?

They are special cookies my family makes. They are called swan cakes.

Swan cakes? Why do you call them swan cakes?

Because anyone who eats them turns into a swan.

What?! Oh, no!

★★★★★★★★★★★

They are called swan cakes.
그들은 백조과자라고 부르지.

Because anyone who eats them turns into a swan.
왜냐하면 그걸 먹는 사람은 누구나 백조로 변하기 때문이지.

next day 다음 날	special 특별한
go(-went-gone) to …로 가다	family 가족
beautiful (날씨가)화창한	make 만들다
sunny 햇빛이 찬란한	call ~을 …라고 부르다
bird 새	swan 백조
sing 노래하다	cake 케이크, 과자
in the trees 나무 속에서	because 왜냐하면
delicious 맛있는	anyone 누구나, 누구든지
cookies 과자	eat 먹다
great 훌륭한, 대단한	turn into …으로 변하다

I'm not an ordinary queen. I'm a powerful witch, and I will turn you all into wild swans.

Suddenly, the boys' arms turned into wings. Their necks grew long and thin. Their noses became black beaks. And white feathers grew all over their bodies.

Now fly away. Fly far, far away!

The eleven swans flew away into the sky. The queen laughed and laughed.

★★★★★★★★★★

ordinary 평범한, 보통의
powerful 강력한, 힘센
witch 마녀
wild swan 야생 백조
suddenly 갑자기
arm 팔
wing 날개
neck 목
grow(-grew-grown) 자라다
long 긴, 기다란
thin 가느다란, 가는
nose 코
become(-became-become) …이 되다
black beak 검은 부리
white feather 하얀 깃털
all over their bodies 몸 전체에
fly(-flew-flown) away 날아가다
far 멀리
into the sky 하늘로
laugh 웃다, 비웃다

I will turn you all into wild swans.
너희들 모두 야생 백조로 만들어 버리겠다.

Their necks grew long and thin.
왕자들의 목은 길고 가느다랗게 자라났습니다.

And white feathers grew all over their bodies.
그리고 몸 전체에 하얀 깃털이 생겨났습니다.

Then she hurried back to the king. She rubbed her eyes and pretended to cry.

Oh, husband, it was terrible. Your sons and I had a picnic by the lake. Then they wanted to go swimming. I told them to wait. You should not swim right after you eat. But they didn't listen. They all jumped into the lake, and they all drowned. It was so terrible.

All my sons are drowned? All my strong, handsome sons? I can't believe it.

I tried to stop them. I'm so sorry.

All my sons are dead. What will I do?

★★★★★★★★★★

I told them to wait. You should not swim right after you eat.
전 아이들에게 식사한 직후에 수영을 해서는 안 된다고 기다리라고 말했어요.

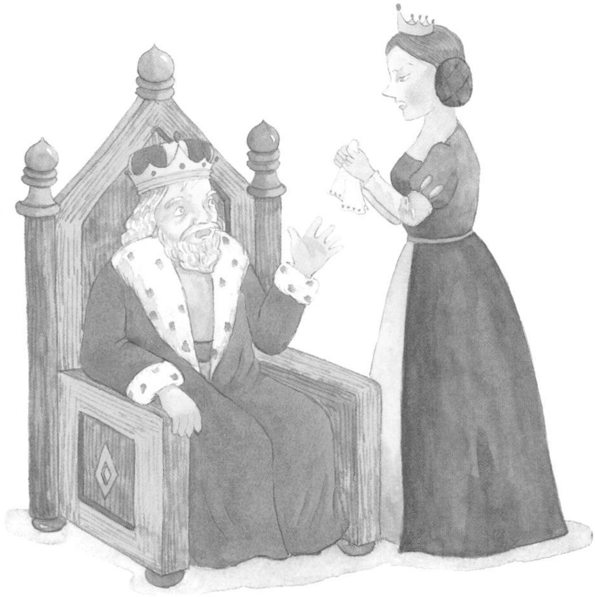

hurry back to
…으로 황급히 돌아가다
rub 비비다, 문지르다
eye 눈
pretend to …인 체하다
husband 남편, 여보
terrible 무서운, 끔찍한
by the lake 호숫가에서
go swimming 수영하러 가다
tell(-told-told) 말하다
right after …한 직후에
listen 귀기울이다
jump into …로 뛰어들다
drown 물에 빠져 죽다, 익사하다
strong 힘센
handsome 잘생긴
believe 믿다
try to …하려 하다
stop 막다, 멈추다
dead 죽은

The king was very sad, but the queen was very happy, for all the children were gone.
Five years passed, and the king became very sick. He called for his servant.

When my sons died, my heart broke. Now I think I am dying. Please bring my daughter, Elise. I want to see her before I die.

Yes, my King.

★★★★★★★★★★

for all the children were gone.
왜냐하면 아이들이 모두 사라졌기 때문이었습니다.

When my sons died, my heart broke.
내 아들들이 죽었을 때 내 가슴은 무너져 내렸도다.

for 왜냐하면
gone 사라진, 죽은
five years 5년
pass 지나가다, 경과하다
sick 아픈
call for …를 큰소리로 부르다
servant 하인, 부하

die 죽다
heart 마음, 가슴
break(-broke-broken)
미어지다, 무너지다
dying 죽어가는
bring 데려오다
before …전에

Elise returned to the castle. Now she was a beautiful young woman. When the queen saw her, she hated her even more. She had a plan to get rid of her.

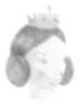

Elise, welcome home. Your father missed you very much. But you are dirty from the road. You must take a bath.

Thank you, Stepmother. But I will only wash my face and hands. I want to see Father soon.

Here. This is walnut juice soap. Use it to clean up.

★★★★★★★★★★

She had a plan to get rid of her.
여왕은 엘리스를 쫓아 버릴 계획을 세웠습니다.

But you are dirty from the road.
그렇지만 너는 여행길로 인해 더러워졌구나.

Use it to clean up. 이것을 사용해서 깨끗이 씻도록 하거라.

return to …로 돌아가다
young woman 젊은 여자
even more 훨씬 더
plan 계획
get rid of 쫓아내다
welcome home 집에 온 것을 환영하다
miss 그리워하다, 보고 싶어하다
dirty 더러운, 지저분한
the road 행로, 여행길
take a bath 목욕하다
stepmother 계모
wash 씻다
face and hands 얼굴과 손
walnut juice soap 호두즙 비누
use 사용하다
clean up 몸을 깨끗이 하다

Elise took the walnut juice soap and washed. The walnut juice made her skin dry and wrinkled. It put dark stains on her face and hands. But Elise did not know it. When her father saw her, he did not recognize her.

Who are you? I want to see my daughter.

It's me, Father. I'm Elise.

You can't trick me. My daughter is young and beautiful. You are ugly and wrinkled. Go away! I don't want to see you.

take(-took-taken) 가져가다
skin 피부
dry 마른, 건조한
wrinkled 주름진
put (어떤 상태로)만들다
dark stains 검은 얼룩
recognize 알아보다
trick 속이다, 장난치다

★★★★★★★★★★★

The walnut juice made her skin dry and wrinkled.
호두즙이 엘리스의 피부를 건조하고 주름지게 만들었습니다.

It put dark stains on her face and hands.
그 호두즙 때문에 엘리스의 얼굴과 손에 시커먼 얼룩들이 생겨났습니다.

When her father saw her, he did not recognize her. 아버지는 엘리스를 보고서도 엘리스를 알아보지 못했습니다.

Elise was so sad. She ran away into the forest. Soon she came to the lake. She looked in the lake and saw her face.

Oh, no! Now I know why Father was so angry. I don't look like me.

Elise washed off the walnut juice in the lake. Soon, she looked young again, and all the stains were gone.

so 너무나
sad 슬픈
run away 달아나다, 도망치다
into the forest 숲 속으로
soon 곧
come to …에 다다르다
look in …안을 들여다보다
see(-saw-seen) 보다
know 알다
angry 화난
look like …처럼 보이다
wash off 씻어내다
again 다시, 또
gone 사라진, 가버린

★★★★★★★★★★★

Now I know why Father was so angry.
이제야 아버지께서 왜 그렇게 화내셨는지 알겠어.

Soon, she looked young again, and all the stains were gone.
엘리스는 금새 다시 젊어졌고 모든 얼룩도 사라졌습니다.

Comprehension

Checkup II

I True or False

1. The queen was also a powerful witch.
2. The king thought he was dying.
3. The queen was happy to see Elise again.
4. The king recognized Elise.
5. Elise washed off the walnut juice in the lake.

II Multiple Choice

1. What did the queen tell the king?

- **a.** She told him that his sons turned into swans.
- **b.** She told him that his sons ran away.
- **c.** She told him that his sons drowned.

2. Who did the king want to see when he was sick?

- **a.** He wanted to see his sons.
- **b.** He wanted to see his daughter.
- **c.** He wanted to see his wife.

정답은 p.117에

3. What did the queen tell Elise?

a. She told her that her brothers were dead.

b. She told her to take a bath.

c. She told her to see the king.

4. What did the walnut soap do to Elise?

a. It put dark stains on her face and hands.

b. It made her skin soft and pretty.

c. It didn't do anything.

5. Where did Elise run to?

a. She ran into the forest.

b. She ran back to Aunt Mina's house.

c. She ran to her room.

III Fill in the Blanks - use the words in the word bank

(each word is used once)

after	cry	face	family	lake
now	rubbed	special	swim	young

1. They are _____ cookies my _____ makes.
2. She _____ her eyes and pretended to _____.
3. You should not _____ right _____ you eat.
4. _____, she was a beautiful _____ woman.
5. She looked in the _____ and saw her _____.

정답은 p.117에

IV Draw a line to connect the first half of each sentence with the second half:

A	B
The day •	• grew long and thin.
The swan cakes •	• was beautiful and sunny.
The boys' arms •	• became black beaks.
The boys' necks •	• turned into wings.
The boys' noses •	• turn people into swans.

SH-03-C
MP3

Chapter 3

She sat by the lake and thought about what to do next. Then she heard someone singing. She walked along the lake and saw an old woman picking berries and singing.

Hello, ma'am. What are you doing here?

Hello, miss. I am waiting for the swans to come.

Swans? What swans?

Every year, a flock of eleven swans comes to this lake. They are so beautiful, and they have golden crowns on their heads. They will come here soon. Oh, there they are!

sit(-sat-sat) by ··· 옆에 앉다
think(-thought-thought) about
··· 에 대해 생각하다
next 다음에
hear(-heard-heard) 듣다
someone 누군가, 어떤 사람
walk along ··· 을 따라 걷다
pick berries 딸기를 따다
ma'am (부인에 대한 존칭)아주머니
miss 아가씨, 처녀
wait for ··· 을 기다리다
every year 매년, 해마다
a flock of 한 무리의
golden crowns 황금관

★★★★★★★★★★

She walked along the lake and saw an old woman picking berries and singing.
엘리스는 호수를 따라 걷다가 한 노파가 딸기를 따면서 노래를 부르고 있는 것을 보았습니다.

Eleven swans flew down to the lake. They were as white as new snow, and they had small, golden crowns on their heads. The biggest swan saw Elise on the lake shore. Then all the swans swam over to her and bowed their heads.

It looks like they know you.

But I don't know them. This is very strange.

I must go home. The sun is going down.

Please wait with me. Something is happening to the swans.

★★★★★★★★★★★

They were as white as new snow.
백조들은 막 내린 눈처럼 새하얗게 빛났습니다.

Then all the swans swam over to her and bowed their heads.
그리고 나서 백조들은 모두 엘리스에게로 헤엄쳐 와서 고개를 숙여 인사했습니다.

It looks like they know you. 백조들이 마치 당신을 아는 것 같군요.

eleven 십일(11)
fly(-flew-flown) down
 날아 내려오다
as white as …만큼 하얀
new snow 막 내린 눈
small 작은
biggest (big의 최상급)가장 큰
see(-saw-seen) 보다
lake shore 호숫가
swim(-swam-swum) over
 헤엄쳐 넘어오다
bow (머리를)숙이다
look like … 처럼 보이다
strange 이상한
must …해야만 한다
sun 태양
something 어떤 것, 무언가
happen to …에게 일어나다

The sun disappeared behind the mountain. Suddenly, the swans became eleven handsome princes.

My brothers! You are alive!

Yes, Elise. The queen put an evil spell on us. In the day, we are swans. At night, we are princes again.

We come to this lake every year.
We hoped to find you some day.

Please take me with you. Don't leave me with the queen.

★★★★★★★★★★★

The queen put an evil spell on us.
여왕이 우리에게 사악한 마법을 걸었단다.

We hoped to find you some day.
우린 언젠가는 널 찾을 수 있기를 바랬어.

Don't leave me with the queen.
절 여왕과 함께 두고 떠나지 말아요.

disappear 사라지다
behind the mountain 산 뒤로
suddenly 갑자기
prince 왕자
alive 살아 있는
put a spell on
…에게 마법을 걸다
evil 사악한

in the day 낮에는
at night 밤에는
every year 매년, 해마다
find 찾다
some day 언젠가
take 데려가다
leave 내버려 두다, 떠나다

Let’s build a big net. Then we can carry Elise with us.

Old woman, please find our father, the king. Tell him that his sons are alive. Tell him to keep hoping. I will try to help them break the spell.

I will. Good luck, miss.

let's …하자
build(-built -built) 만들다
big net 커다란 그물
carry 옮기다, 나르다
tell 말하다
keep hoping 계속 희망을 갖다
try to …하려 하다
help 돕다
break the spell 마법을 풀다
good luck 행운을 빌다

★★★★★★★★★★★

Tell him that his sons are alive.
아버지께 아들들이 모두 살아 있다고 말씀드려 주세요.

I will try to help them break the spell.
전 마법을 풀 수 있도록 오빠들을 도울게요.

The brothers built a big net to carry Elise. When the morning came, they all turned into swans again. Elise got in the net. The swans picked her up and flew away with her. They flew for many hours. Finally, they came to a cave by a different lake. The swans landed in front of the cave.

build(-built-built) 만들다
morning 아침
turn into … 으로 변하다
get(-got-gotten) in
… 에 올라타다
pick up 들어올리다
fly(-flew-flown) away
날아가다
for many hours 수많은 시간 동안
finally 마침내, 드디어
cave 동굴
by a different lake
또 다른 호숫가에
land 착륙하다, 내리다
in front of … 앞에

★★★★★★★★★★

The brothers built a big net to carry Elise.
오빠들은 엘리스를 옮길 커다란 그물을 만들었습니다.

The swans picked her up and flew away with her.
백조들은 엘리스를 들어올려서 날아갔습니다.

When the sun set, they became her brothers again.

This is where we live now.

It is not as nice as the castle, but we like it.

There are berries and fruit trees in the forest.

You should get some sleep now.

Yes, I am tired. I hope I can find how to save you.

Maybe you will dream it. Good night, Elise.

set (해가)지다
become(-became-become)
  … 이 되다
as nice as … 만큼 좋은
castle 성
berries (berry의 복수)딸기
fruit trees 과일 나무
get some sleep 잠자다
tired 피곤한, 지친
how to … 하는 방법
save 구하다
maybe 아마도
dream 꿈꾸다
good night (저녁인사)잘 자

★★★★★★★★★★

This is where we live now.
이곳이 현재 우리가 사는 곳이란다.

I hope I can find how to save you.
제가 오빠들을 구할 수 있는 방법을 찾을 수 있기를 바래요.

That night, Elise had a dream. A fairy came to her and told her how to break the spell.

This nettle grows outside the cave. Pick the nettles and crush them with your feet. Make the nettles into thread. Then weave the thread into eleven coats. Throw the coats over your brothers, and they will never be swans again. The spell will be broken. But be careful. You must not speak a word before the spell is broken. If you say anything at all to anyone, your brothers will never be saved.

★★★★★★★★★★★

You must not speak a word before the spell is broken.
너는 마법이 풀리기 전까지는 한 마디도 해서는 안 된다.

If you say anything at all to anyone, your brothers will never be saved. 만약 네가 누군가에게 어떤 말이든 한다면 절대로 너의 오빠들을 구할 수 없을 것이다.

night 밤
fairy 요정
tell(-told-told) 말하다
nettle 쐐기풀
grow 자라다, 성장하다
outside the cave 동굴 밖에서
pick 따다
crush 으깨다, 부수다
feet 발
make into … 으로 만들다
thread 실
weave 엮다, 짜다
coat 코트
throw over … 너머로 던지다
broken 풀린, 깨진
careful 조심하는, 주의 깊은
speak a word 한 마디하다
anything 무언가, 무엇이든
anyone 누군가, 아무도

The next morning, Elise was very happy. She knew how to save her brothers. She ran outside and found the nettles. She picked many nettles and carried them to the cave. Then she crushed the nettles with her feet until they were soft. Then she made thread and began to weave the first coat. She was still working when the sun went down.

next morning 다음 날 아침
happy 행복한, 즐거운
know(-knew-known) 알다
how to …하는 방법
run outside 밖으로 달려나가다
find(-found-found) 찾다
many 많은
carry 옮기다, 나르다
until …할 때까지
soft 부드러운
begin(-began-begun) to …하기 시작하다
first 첫번째
still 여전히, 아직도
work 일하다
sun 태양
go(-went-gone) down (해가)지다

★★★★★★★★★★

she crushed the nettles with her feet until they were soft.
엘리스는 쐐기풀이 부드러워질 때까지 발로 으깨었습니다.

She was still working when the sun went down.
엘리스는 해가 졌을 때도 여전히 일을 하고 있었습니다.

Her brothers came home and saw her working.

Hi, Elise. What are you doing?

But Elise didn't answer. She was not allowed to speak. She smiled at her brothers and showed them the nettle coat.

come home 집에 오다
hi 안녕
answer 대답하다
be allowed to
(… 하는 것이) 허락되다
speak 말하다
smile at
(… 에게) 미소를 짓다
show 보여 주다
coat 코트

★★★★★★★★★★★

She was not allowed to speak.
엘리스는 말을 못하게 되어 있었습니다.

She smiled at her brothers and showed them the nettle coat.
엘리스는 오빠들에게 미소를 지으며 쐐기풀 코트를 보여 주었습니다.

What's wrong? Why won't you talk to us?

She's making a strange coat. Maybe the coats will break the spell.

That is why she cannot speak. If she speaks, the magic coats will not work.

Elise smiled again. Her brothers were so smart. They helped her when they could. They brought her food and water, so she could work on the magic coats. After a few days, the first coat was done. Elise and her brothers were very happy.

wrong 잘못된, 문제가 있는
won't will not의 줄임말
talk to … 에게 말하다
us (we의 목적격)우리를[에게]
make 만들다
strange 이상한
maybe 아마도
break the spell 마법을 풀다
magic 마법의

work on 효과가 있다, 작용하다
일을 계속하다
smart 영리한
help 돕다
bring(-brought-brought) 가져오다
food 음식
water 물
after a few days 수일 후에
done 끝난, 마친

★★★★★★★★★★★

Why won't you talk to us?
어째서 우리에게 말을 하지 않는 거니?

If she speaks, the magic coats will not work.
만일 엘리스가 말을 하면 마법 코트가 효력을 잃을 거야.

so she could work on the magic coats.
그래서 엘리스는 마법 코트를 만들 수가 있었습니다.

Checkup III

I True or False

1. The old woman was eating lunch by the lake.
2. The swans turned into Elise's brothers.
3. The old woman did not want to find the king.
4. The brothers lived in a cave.
5. Elise told her brothers about her dream.

II Multiple Choice

1. **What was strange about the eleven swans?**
   a. They had golden crowns on their heads.
   b. They looked like young men.
   c. They liked to pick berries.

2. **How did the princes take Elise with them?**
   a. They turned her into a swan.
   b. They built a big net and carried her.
   c. They found a boat for her.

정답은 p.118에

3. **Who spoke to Elise in her dream?**
   - **a.** A fairy spoke to her.
   - **b.** Her mother spoke to her.
   - **c.** A handsome prince spoke to her.

4. **What is a nettle?**
   - **a.** A nettle is a kind of animal.
   - **b.** A nettle is a kind of plant.
   - **c.** A nettle is a kind of rock.

5. **What must Elise make from the nettles?**
   - **a.** She must make a big net.
   - **b.** She must make dinner.
   - **c.** She must make coats.

Checkup III

III **Fill in the Blanks - use the words in the word bank**
(each word is used once)

berries	came	disappeared	trees	speak
spell	swans	mountain	waiting	working

1. I am _____ for the _____ to come.
2. The sun _____ behind the _____.
3. There are _____ and fruit _____ in the forest.
4. You must not _____ a word before the _____ is broken.
5. Her brothers _____ home and saw her _____.

정답은 p.118에

IV **Draw a line to connect the first half of each sentence with the second half:**

A			B
She ran outside	•	•	and carried them into the cave.
She picked many nettles	•	•	and began to weave.
She crushed the nettles with her feet	•	•	until they were soft.
She made thread	•	•	so she could work.
Her brothers brought her food and water	•	•	and found the nettles.

SH-03-C
MP3

Chapter 4

One day, Elise went outside to pick more nettles. Suddenly, a hunting party appeared. The leader of the hunting party was a handsome young man. He saw Elise, and walked over to her.

one day 어느 날
go(-went-gone) outside
밖으로 나가다
pick 따다, 집다
more nettles 더 많은 쐐기풀
suddenly 갑자기
hunting party 사냥하는 무리
appear 나타나다
leader 지도자, 통솔자
walk over to … 에게 다가가다

★★★★★★★★★★

One day, Elise went outside to pick more nettles.
어느 날, 엘리스는 더 많은 쐐기풀을 따기 위해 밖으로 나갔습니다.

He saw Elise, and walked over to her.
그는 엘리스를 보고 그녀에게로 다가갔습니다.

Hello, miss. I am the king of this land. Who are you?

Elise bowed to the young king, but she did not say anything.

The girl does not speak, my King. What is wrong with her?

I don't know. But she is very beautiful. I will take her to the castle and marry her. She will be a wonderful queen.

miss 아가씨, 처녀
land 나라, 땅
bow to … 에게 머리숙이다
young king 젊은 왕
speak 말하다
wrong 잘못된, 문제가 있는
beautiful 아름다운
take 데려가다
castle 성
marry 결혼하다
wonderful 멋진, 훌륭한
queen 여왕

★★★★★★★★★★★

she did not say anything.
그녀는 아무 말도 하지 않았습니다.

I will take her to the castle and marry her.
그녀를 성으로 데리고 가서 그녀와 결혼할 것이다.

But Elise did not want to go with the young king. She wanted to stay with her brothers and help them. She shook her head no and started to cry. But the king picked her up and put her on his horse.

Do not cry, my dear. This cave is not a good place to live. You will be very happy at my castle.

Soon they arrived at the young king's castle. Everyone welcomed Elise and tried to make her happy. Elise liked the people at the castle, but she was still very sad. One person did not like Elise. The king's chief minister did not trust her.

★★★★★★★★★★★

She shook her head no and started to cry.
그녀는 아니라고 머리를 가로저으면서 울기 시작했습니다.

Everyone welcomed Elise and tried to make her happy.
모든 사람들이 엘리스를 환영했고 즐겁게 해 주려고 애썼습니다.

stay with …와 함께 머물다
shake(-shook-shaken) 흔들다
head 머리
start to …하기 시작하다
cry 울다
pick up 들어올리다
put on …위에 태우다
horse 말
good place 좋은 곳
live 살다
be happy at …에 만족스러운
arrive at …에 도착하다
welcome 환영하다
people 사람들
chief minister 고문관, 수석 대신
trust 믿다, 신뢰하다

My King, this girl is too strange. Why won't she talk to us? And why does she cry all the time? She is not a normal girl. I think she is a witch.

Nonsense, she is not a witch. I think she misses her home. I have an idea to make her happier.

A few days later, the young king showed Elise a special room in the castle.

I made this room to look just like your cave. We even brought your nettles and your coats. You can continue your strange work. Now will you be happy for me?

★★★★★★★★★★

I have an idea to make her happier.
그녀를 더 행복하게 해줄 좋은 생각이 떠올랐소.

I made this room to look just like your cave.
난 이 방을 당신의 동굴과 똑같이 보이도록 만들었다오.

Now will you be happy for me?
자, 이제 나를 위해서 행복한 모습을 보여 주겠소?

all the time 항상, 늘
normal 보통의, 정상의
witch 마녀
nonsense 쓸데없는 소리
miss 그리워하다
happier 더 행복한
a few days later 며칠 뒤
show 보여 주다
special room 특별한 방
look like … 처럼 보이다
even 심지어, … 조차도
bring(-brought-brought) 가져오다
continue 계속하다

For the first time since coming to the castle, Elise smiled. She was so happy. Now she could make more magic coats for her brothers. She hugged the young king and kissed his hand in thanks.
Soon, they were married.
Elise and the king were very happy together. Every day, she ruled the kingdom with the king.

★★★★★★★★★★★

For the first time since coming to the castle,
성에 도착한 이후 처음으로,

She hugged the young king and kissed his hand in thanks.
엘리스는 젊은 왕을 껴안고 감사의 뜻으로 왕의 손에 입을 맞추었습니다.

for the first time 처음으로
since … 이래 [이후]
magic coats 마법 코트
hug 껴안다
kiss 키스하다, 입맞추다
hand 손
in thanks 감사의 뜻으로
marry(-married-married)
결혼하다
every day 매일
rule 통치하다, 다스리다
kingdom 왕국

Every night, she worked on the magic coats. But the chief minister still did not trust her. He watched her every night. One night, Elise ran out of nettles. She left the castle to pick more. The chief minister followed her. He saw her picking the nettles, but he did not know why.

This is too strange. A normal girl does not pick nettles in the middle of the night. Now I can prove that she is a witch. The king will put her in jail.

every night 매일 밤
work on 일을 계속하다
trust 믿다, 신뢰하다
watch 지켜보다
run out of …이 떨어지다
nettles 쐐기풀
leave(-left-left) 떠나다
pick more 더 많이 따다
follow 뒤따라가다
normal 보통의, 정상의
in the middle of the night 한밤중에
prove 증명하다
put in jail 감옥에 가두다

★★★★★★★★★★★

He saw her picking the nettles, but he did not know why.
그는 엘리스가 쐐기풀을 따는 것을 보았지만 그 이유를 몰랐습니다.

The next morning, the chief minister found the young king.

My King, I can prove your wife is a witch. Last night, I followed her. She left the castle and went to the cave. She picked lots of nettles to make those strange coats. A normal girl does not pick nettles in the middle of the night. She is a witch.

I don't believe you. My wife is wonderful. I love her. She is not a witch.

Please, let me show you. Watch her at night. You will see.

Alright, I will watch her. Then I will prove that she is not a witch.

★★★★★★★★★★

She picked lots of nettles to make those strange coats.
그녀는 그 이상한 코트를 만들기 위해서 많은 쐐기풀을 땄습니다.

Please, let me show you.
제가 보여드리겠습니다.

next morning 다음 날 아침
find (-found-found) 찾다
last night 지난 밤
lots of 많은
believe 믿다
wife 아내, 부인

let …하게 하다
show 보여 주다
at night 밤에
see 보다, 알다
alright 알았다

For many nights, the young king and the chief minister watched Elise. She worked hard weaving the magic coats. Finally, ten coats were finished. But she needed more nettles. That night, Elise left the castle and went to the cave. The king and the chief minister followed her. They watched her picking nettles under the moon.

for many nights 며칠 밤 동안
work hard 열심히 일하다
weave 짜다, 엮다
finally 마침내, 드디어
finish 끝내다, 마치다
need 필요하다
cave 동굴
follow 뒤따르다
under the moon 달빛 아래에서

★★★★★★★★★★

She worked hard weaving the magic coats.
그녀는 열심히 마법 코트를 짰습니다.

They watched her picking nettles under the moon.
그들은 달빛 아래에서 엘리스가 쐐기풀을 따는 것을 지켜보았습니다.

Now do you see? Only a witch picks nettles at night. She will cast spells on the kingdom.

This is terrible. But I must believe you. Oh, how sad I am. My beautiful wife is a witch.

Will you put her in jail?

Yes, I will. I must protect my kingdom. I will tell the guards to arrest her tomorrow morning.

only 단지, 오직
cast a spell on
(…에게)마법을 걸다
kingdom 왕국
terrible 끔찍한, 무서운
must …해야만 한다
believe 믿다
how 참으로, 얼마나
put in jail 감옥에 가두다
protect 보호하다
guard 경비병
arrest 체포하다
tomorrow morning 내일 아침

★★★★★★★★★★★

She will cast spells on the kingdom.
그녀는 저희 왕국에 마법을 걸 것입니다.

I will tell the guards to arrest her tomorrow morning.
내일 아침 그녀를 체포하도록 경비병에게 명할 것이오.

Comprehension

Checkup IV

I True or False

1. Elise said hello to the young king.
2. Elise wanted to stay in the cave.
3. The chief minister wanted to marry Elise.
4. The chief minister saw Elise picking nettles.
5. The king decided to put Elise in jail.

II Multiple Choice

1. **Who was the leader of the hunting party?**
   a. The chief huntsman
   b. The chief minister
   c. The king of the land

2. **Why did the chief minister think Elise was a witch?**
   a. Because she was so beautiful.
   b. Because she was so smart.
   c. Because she was so strange.

정답은 p.119에

3. How did the king try to make Elise happier?

a. He made a room to look just like the cave.

b. He took her back to the cave.

c. He brought her brothers to the castle.

4. What did Elise do every night?

a. She ruled the kingdom with the king.

b. She worked on the magic coats.

c. She turned into a swan.

5. Why did the chief minister watch Elise every night?

a. Because he wanted to prove that she was a witch.

b. Because he wanted to help her make magic coats.

c. Because he wanted to be the king.

Checkup IV

III Fill in the Blanks - use the words in the word bank
(each word is used once)

cave	finished	kissed	left	make
place	welcomed	ten	went	young

1. This _____ is not a good _____ to live.
2. Everyone _____ Elise and tried to _____ her happy.
3. She hugged the _____ king and _____ his hand in thanks.
4. She _____ the castle and _____ to the cave.
5. Finally, _____ coats were _____.

정답은 p.119에

IV Draw a line to connect the words that are opposites of each other:

A		B
King	•	• Girl
Son	•	• Mother
Father	•	• Wife
Husband	•	• Daughter
Boy	•	• Queen

SH-03-C
MP3

Chapter 5

The next morning, the guards arrested Elise. They took her to a tall tower and locked her in a small room. They threw the nettles and coats at her.

Here are your nettles. They will be your pillow.

Here are your coats. They will be your blankets.

Good bye, witch. Don't cast your evil spells on us.

take(-took-taken) 데려가다
tall 높은, 키가 큰
tower 탑
lock 가두다, 잠그다
small room 조그만 방
throw(-threw-thrown) 던지다
pillow 베개
blanket 담요
good bye (작별인사) 안녕
evil 사악한, 못된

★★★★★★★★★★★

They took her to a tall tower and locked her in a small room.
경비병들은 엘리스를 높은 탑으로 끌고 가서 조그만 방에 가두어 버렸습니다.

Don't cast your evil spells on us.
당신의 사악한 마법을 우리에게 걸지 마시오.

Elise was so sad. She loved the young king, but he thought she was a witch. She began to cry. Suddenly, she heard birds flying by the window. She looked outside and saw eleven swans. The swans all had golden crowns on their heads. Her brothers found her! She pointed to the jail house. The biggest swan nodded his head. He understood what was happening. Now Elise had new hope. She started to work very hard on the last coat. She worked all day and all night long. She didn't sleep or eat anything.

★★★★★★★★★★★

Suddenly, she heard birds flying by the window.
갑자기 엘리스는 창가에서 새들이 날아다니는 소리를 들었습니다.

She started to work very hard on the last coat.
엘리스는 마지막 코트를 열심히 짜기 시작했습니다.

She didn't sleep or eat anything.
엘리스는 자지도 않았고 아무것도 먹지 않았습니다.

begin(-began-begun) to
… 하기 시작하다
cry 울다
suddenly 갑자기
hear(-heard-heard) 듣다
bird 새
fly 날다
by the window 창가로[에]
golden crowns 금관
point to … 을 가리키다
jail house 감옥 건물
biggest 가장 큰

nod 고개를 끄덕이다
understand (-understood-understood)
이해하다
happen 발생하다, 일어나다
new hope 새로운 희망
start to … 하기 시작하다
last 마지막
all day and all night long
밤낮으로 줄곧
sleep 잠자다
eat 먹다

The next morning, the young king arrived with the chief minister.

Good morning, witch. Today you will go to jail. Are you ready?

Please speak to us. Tell us why you are making these strange coats. If we knew why, you would not go to jail.

arrive 도착하다
chief minister 고문관, 수석 대신
today 오늘
go to jail 감옥에 가다
ready 준비된
speak to … 에게 말하다
know(-knew-known) 알다

★★★★★★★★★★

Tell us why you are making these strange coats.
당신이 왜 이러한 이상한 코트를 만들고 있는지 우리에게 말해 보시오.

If we knew why, you would not go to jail.
만일 우리가 그 이유를 알면 당신은 감옥에 가지 않아도 되오.

But Elise did not say anything. She looked at the king with a sad face.

She will not speak. We must send her to jail.

I'm so sorry, my dear. But I must protect my kingdom.

Elise picked up the eleven magic coats. The last coat was almost finished. She followed the chief minister to a cart.

This cart will take you to jail. Get in.

say 말하다
look at …을 보다
with a sad face 슬픈 얼굴로
must …해야만 한다
send to jail 감옥으로 보내다
sorry 미안한, 죄송한
protect 보호하다
kingdom 왕국
pick up 집어들다
almost 거의
finish 끝내다, 마치다
follow 뒤따르다
cart 수레
get in 타다

★★★★★★★★★★

The last coat was almost finished.
마지막 코트가 거의 완성되었습니다.

She followed the chief minister to a cart.
엘리스는 고문관을 따라 마차로 갔습니다.

This cart will take you to jail.
이 마차는 당신을 감옥까지
데려다 줄 것이오.

Elise got into the cart. She quickly started working on the last coat. She hoped to finish the coat quickly. The cart rolled through the town. All the townspeople came out to see Elise go to jail. They arrived at the jail house just as Elise finished the last coat. The guards opened the cart door and Elise stepped out. Suddenly, eleven swans flew down to her. She threw a coat over each swan. The spell was broken, and the swans turned into her brothers.

get(-got-gotten) into 안에 타다
quickly 재빨리
start working on
계속 만들기 시작하다
hope to … 하기를 바라다
through the town 마을을 지나서
townspeople 마을 사람들
come out 나오다

arrive at … 에 도착하다
step 걸음을 옮기다, 발을 내딛다
fly(-flew-flown) down 날아앉다
throw(-threw-thrown) over
… 너머로 던지다
spell 주문
broken 깨진, 풀린
turn into … 으로 변하다

★★★★★★★★★★★

All the townspeople came out to see Elise go to jail. 마을 사람들 모두가 엘리스가 감옥에 가는 것을 보려고 나왔습니다.

They arrived at the jail house just as Elise finished the last coat. 그들은 엘리스가 마지막 코트를 막 완성했을 때 감옥에 도착했습니다.

She is a witch! She turned those swans into young men!

No, I am not a witch. These young men are my brothers.

Elise is right. Our stepmother was a witch. She cast an evil spell on us. The nettle coats broke the spell. Now we are free.

Why didn't you tell us this before?

I could not speak while I worked on the coats. If I said a word to anyone, the magic coats would not work. I'm sorry I worried you.

You were so brave and strong. I love you, Elise.

I love you too. I'm so happy I can speak to you now.

witch 마녀
right 맞는, 옳은
stepmother 계모
cast a spell on
…에게 마법을 걸다
break(-broke-broken) 깨뜨리다
free 자유로운, 풀려난
before 이전에
while …하는 동안
say(-said-said) a word
한 마디 말을 하다
worry 걱정시키다
brave 용감한
strong 힘센, 강한

★★★★★★★★★★★

I could not speak while I worked on the coats.
코트를 만들 동안에는 말을 할 수가 없었어요.

If I said a word to anyone, the magic coats would not work.
만일 제가 누군가에게 한 마디라도 한다면 마법의 코트는 효력을 잃어요.

I'm so happy I can speak to you now.
이젠 당신에게 말을 할 수가 있어서 너무나 기뻐요.

Elise, her brothers and the young king went back to the castle. They sent a messenger to Elise's father. The next day, he came to see his children.

Elise! My sons! I'm so happy to see you again.

Father, I missed you so much. Where is Stepmother?

I don't know. Your messenger told me about the evil spell. I sent my guards to arrest her. But when they went to her rooms, she was gone. I hope we never see her again.

★★★★★★★★★★★★

I sent my guards to arrest her.
난 그녀를 체포하도록 경비병들을 보냈단다.

But when they went to her rooms, she was gone.
하지만 경비병들이 그녀의 방에 갔을 때 그녀는 사라지고 없더구나.

go(-went-gone) back to
… 으로 돌아가다
send(-sent-sent) 보내다
messenger 전령
next day 다음 날
children 자식들, 아이들
miss 그리워하다, 보고 싶어하다
arrest 체포하다
gone 사라진
hope 희망하다, 바라다
never 결코 … 않다

That night, the young king held a grand party. Everyone had a wonderful time. And they all lived happily ever after.

that night 그 날 밤
hold(-held-held) 베풀다, 개최하다
grand party 성대한 파티
everyone 모든 사람
live 살다
happily 행복하게
ever after 이후 내내

★★★★★★★★★★★

And they all lived happily ever after.
그리고 그들 모두가 이후 내내 행복하게 잘 살았습니다.

Checkup V

I True or False

1. The guards did not give Elise her nettles and coats.
2. Elise's brothers found her.
3. Elise finished the eleven coats.
4. When the spell was broken, the eleven brothers turned back into swans.
5. Elise was happy because she could speak to the king.

II Multiple Choice

1. Where did the guards take Elise?

a. They took her to the cave.
b. They took her to her father's castle.
c. They took her to a small room in a tall tower.

2. Why did the king send Elise to jail?

a. Because he had to protect his kingdom.
b. Because he did not like nettles.
c. Because Elise did not give him a coat.

Word List

다음은 이 책에 나오는 단어와 숙어를 수록한 것입니다.
* 표는 중학교 영어 교육 과정의 기본 어휘입니다.

A

B

C

D

Q

R

S

T

Notes

Story House

03. The Wild Swans 백조왕자

펴낸이	임 병 업
펴낸곳	(주)월드컴 에듀
등록	2000년 1월 17일
주소	서울특별시 강남구 언주로 120 인스토피아 빌딩 912호
전화	02)3273-4300(대표)
팩스	02)3273-4303
홈페이지	www.wcbooks.co.kr
이메일	wc4300@wcbooks.co.kr